THE XTREME TEAM

## DATE DUE

| | | | |
|---|---|---|---|
| | | | |
| | | | |
| | | | |
| | | | |
| | | | |
| | | | |
| | | | |
| | | | |
| | | | |
| | | | |
| | | | |
| | | | |
| | | | |
| | | | |
| | | | |
| | | | |
| | | | |
| | | | |

D1280266

DEMCO 38-297

# MATT CHRISTOPHER®

# #3
# ROLLER HOCKEY RUMBLE

Text by **Stephanie Peters**
Illustrated by **Michael Koelsch**

**LITTLE, BROWN AND COMPANY**

New York ❧ Boston

Little, Brown and Company

Time Warner Book Group
1271 Avenue of the Americas, New York, NY 10020
Visit our Web site at www.lb-kids.com

First Edition

The characters and events portrayed in this book are fictitious. Any similarity to real persons, living or dead, is coincidental and not intended by the author.

Matt Christopher® is a registered trademark
of Catherine M. Christopher.

Library of Congress Cataloging-in-Publication Data
Peters, Stephanie True.
Roller hockey rumble / text by Stephanie Peters ; illustrated by Michael Koelsch. — 1st ed.
    p.    cm. — (The extreme team ; #3)
"Matt Christopher."
Summary: When Bizz and her friends arrange a high-stakes roller hockey game with another team, Bizz is reminded about the importance of friendship.
ISBN 0-316-73754-2 (hc) / ISBN 0-316-73755-0 (pb)
[1. Roller hockey — Fiction.    2. Friendship — Fiction.]
I. Koelsch, Michael, ill.    II. Christopher, Matt.
III. Title.    IV. Series.
PZ7.P441833Ro 2004                    2003054500
[Fic] — dc21

10    9    8    7    6    5    4    3    2    1

WOR (hc)

COM-MO (pb)

Printed in the United States of America

# CHAPTER ONE

'Hey, dudes, what's up?" Belicia "Bizz" Juarez swooped into the park and braked her inline skates to a stop in front of Jonas Malloy and Charlie Abbott. "Why aren't you riding the ramps and rails?"

Jonas shook his head. "They're crammed full of newbies," he said glumly. "It's Beginner's Day, remember?"

Bizz's face fell. "Oh, yeah," she said. Beginner's Day was when kids still learning about inline skating and other extreme sports — newbies — got the skatepark all to themselves. Newbies were paired with older, experienced skaters who watched over them as they tried out different equipment and moves.

Bizz had nothing against kids improving their skills. She just wished they wouldn't get in her way when she wanted to skate!

Jonas shaded his eyes against the bright November sun and pointed. "Hey, isn't that Savannah by the pyramid, with Alison?"

Bizz followed his gaze. Sure enough, Savannah Smith stood next to the pyramid ramp. She checked her inlines, then skated hard up one slope of the pyramid. When she reached the top, she gave a little hop, made a quarter turn in midair, and rolled down another slope. Alison Lee, the teenager who watched over the skatepark, applauded.

"What's Savannah doing out there on Beginner's Day?" Charlie asked. Charlie, a newcomer to town, was still getting to know the other kids. "I thought she was a good skater already."

"She *is,*" Bizz replied loyally. "She's *way* better than those newbies out there! I'm going to rescue her." Bizz took off full tilt to the pyramid.

"Yo, Bizz, hold up." Alison stepped in front of

Bizz. "You know you're not supposed to be out here today."

"I'll clear out in a sec," Bizz said, "but I'm taking Savannah with me. She's too good to be out here!"

"Thanks, Bizz," Savannah said quietly. "But I'd really like to stay and practice. Alison's teaching me a lot and —"

Bizz cut her off. "You've got better things to do!"

"Like what?" Alison wanted to know.

"Like — like —" Bizz looked around. Her gaze landed on the park's roller hockey rink. It was empty. "Like play roller hockey with me and the guys, that's what!"

"Roller hockey?" Savannah sounded doubtful.

"Sure! We can use the park's hockey equipment, can't we, Alison?"

Alison sighed. "That's what it's there for."

Bizz grabbed Savannah's hand. "Then what're we waiting for? Look" — she pointed to where Jonas and Charlie had been joined by Xavier "X" McSweeney and Mark Goldstein — "the rest of the crew is here.

3

We can play three-on-three, no goalies. It'll be a blast." Before Savannah could protest, Bizz pulled her away from Alison and the newbies.

"Don't forget to sign up for rink time!" Alison called out after them.

Minutes later, the two girls and four boys skated onto the roller hockey rink. Each carried a light-weight hockey stick and wore a helmet with a clear face mask. They had gloves on their hands and pads on their elbows and knees. Everyone but Savannah put mouth guards in.

Savannah eyed the hard rubber hockey puck anxiously. "I don't have a mouth guard," she said. "Maybe I should just watch."

"We'll be careful," Bizz reassured her. "Savannah, you team up with Jonas and X. Charlie and Mark are with me." She tightened the strap under her helmet. "Game on!"

# CHAPTER TWO

Bizz faced off against Jonas. With the puck between them, she and Jonas tapped their sticks together three times, then attacked.

Bizz freed the disk and passed it quickly to Charlie. Charlie caught it on his stick and started to dribble toward the goal. Savannah skated to get in front of him. Charlie flicked the puck right under her stick, dodged around her, and made a break for the empty goal. Jonas and X tried to intercept, but neither reached him in time. Charlie shot — and scored!

Bizz cheered, then skated over to Savannah. "Sorry, I forgot to tell you to keep your stick blade on the ground," she said. "That way, you'll be ready to stop the puck if it comes near you. Okay?" Savannah nodded, and Bizz skated back for the next face-off.

This time, Jonas got control. Instead of passing, he took off like a shot toward the goal. Bizz chased him. Charlie streaked down next to her. Mark shifted nervously in front of the goal — and the fast-approaching Jonas.

"Stop him! Stop him!" Bizz yelled.

Mark's eyes grew wide, but he skated forward and tried to put his body between Jonas and the goal. Moments before a collision, Jonas pulled up short and passed the puck to X. X deflected it into the goal. Mark spun to see what had happened, lost his balance, and fell.

Bizz skated a wide circle behind the goal, then dug the puck out of the net. As she passed Mark, she reached a hand down to help him up. "Good job standing your ground against Jonas," she said, adding with a grin, "Now if you could just stand your ground the rest of the game . . ."

"Ha, ha," Mark said. He took her hand and struggled to his feet.

Bizz won the third face-off. She looked up to see Savannah standing close to the goal. "It's all yours, amiga!" She slapped a hard pass to her friend. But instead of stopping on Savannah's blade, the puck bounced off and skittered over the sideline.

Bizz retrieved it, then skated up next to Savannah. "Sorry, my fault again," she said. "I should have told you to keep your stick soft when you get a pass. You know, kind of cushion the puck a bit to control it. Next time, okay?"

"Got it," Savannah said. The girls slapped high fives and went back to their spots.

For the next ten minutes, the two teams traded goals, joking and teasing one another the whole time. Bizz continued to offer Savannah pointers.

"Will you stop helping the enemy?" Jonas said at one point.

"Enemy-schnenemy," Bizz retorted. "She's a roller hockey newbie. I'm just cuttin' her some slack."

"Speaking of slack, I gotta take a break," Mark said. He took off his helmet. "Anybody want to hit the water fountain in the Community Center with me?"

It turned out that everyone else was thirsty, too. Together, they skated to the center and drank big gulps of cold water.

"All right," Bizz said as they started back toward the rink. "Everybody ready for round two?" But when they reached the rink, it was no longer empty. A boy was there taking shots on goal.

Bizz skated over to the newcomer. He looked a little older than she was.

"Excuse me," she said politely, "we're in the middle of a game."

The boy slowly turned. "Excuse *me,*" he sneered. "When I got here, the rink was empty. And there weren't any names on the sign-up sheet. Well, *now* there's a name. Mine."

He turned away, raised his stick behind him, and slammed in another shot.

# CHAPTER THREE

Bubbles of fury rose inside Bizz. Some of her anger was at the boy's rudeness — but the rest was at herself. She'd completely forgotten to sign up, even though Alison had reminded her to do it. The boy had every right to be there. More, since he'd signed up for the time.

Then she had an idea. "Listen," she said to the boy, "you wanna play with us? We're going three-on-three, just goofing around and having fun. What do you say?"

The boy glanced over at the others. "Pretty motley-lookin' crew," he said with a sniff. "I'll have to tone down my game to play at your level."

*Don't do us any favors,* Bizz wanted to say. But instead, she gritted her teeth and replied, "I'm Bizz."

"Frank," the boy snapped.

X offered to give Frank his spot.

"Fine, but I'll take the face-off," Frank said, shouldering Jonas aside. Jonas frowned, but skated back next to Savannah.

*This guy's a real bully,* Bizz thought angrily as she readied herself for the face-off. *Well, he better not cause trouble.*

Her anger cranked up another notch a moment later. Frank won the face-off and immediately fired a pass at Savannah. Savannah, caught off guard, bobbled the puck. It rolled on its edge until Charlie swooped in, scooped it up, and shot it straight into the goal.

Frank skated over to Savannah. "Whatsa matter with you?" he bellowed. The way he loomed over her, he looked like a grizzly bear standing on its hind legs.

Savannah shrank back. "S-sorry," she stammered.

Frank rolled his eyes and skated back to the face-off circle. "'Sorry,' she says. Oh, brother."

"Give her a break. She's still learning how to play hockey," Bizz shot back.

"That right?" Frank draped his hockey stick across his shoulders and rested his arms on it. "Well, maybe she shouldn't be out here, then. Maybe none of you should. You oughta leave the rink open to people who really know how to play."

"People like you, you mean?" Bizz finally let her anger out full force.

"Yeah, me and my team," Frank said.

Bizz spread her hands wide. "Team? What team? I don't see anybody here but you." By now, the others had gathered behind her. "You, and my buds here, that is."

Frank drew himself up tall. "Oh, I've got a team, all right. And we'd *crush* you guys in a heartbeat!"

"Ha!" Bizz let out a harsh laugh. "Wanna bet?"

Frank slowly smiled. "Sure, I'll bet," he said in a nasty voice. "I bet we beat you guys in a game next Saturday. Ten o'clock. Winner takes all."

"Takes all of what?" Charlie wanted to know.

Frank looked around at the rink and nodded. "This place beats where my team's been playing. So let's say whichever team wins gets to use this rink whenever they want. The losers clear out when the winners show up, no matter what. Deal?"

Bizz didn't hesitate. "Deal!" she cried, sticking out her hand. Frank spat on his hand and shook hers. Bizz pulled her hand away and wiped it on her pants. "Gross," she muttered.

Frank laughed, gathered up his gear, and skated away. "See you next Saturday, lo-o-o-o-o-sers!" he called over his shoulder.

"What a jerk," Bizz said, turning to look at her friends.

They were all staring at her.

"Uh, guys? Is something wrong?"

# CHAPTER FOUR

"Is something *wrong?*" X repeated. "Yeah, there's something *wrong!*"

"You just bet the roller hockey rink!" Jonas exploded.

A hot flush crept into Bizz's face. It suddenly dawned on her that her friends might have wanted to talk over the bet before she agreed to it.

Then she shook herself. "What are you guys worried about?" she asked, filling her voice with confidence. "We'll win, and that guy won't bother us again!"

"But if we lose, he'll be in our faces all the time," Charlie said, shaking his head.

Mark agreed. "Guys like him rub your nose in it when you lose."

Bizz picked up her hockey stick. "Well, then we'll just have to be sure we don't lose. Now, who's ready to play?"

But no one seemed to have much interest in playing anymore. After ten minutes, Mark called it quits.

"Yeah, I'm done, too," Charlie said, popping out his mouth guard. The others started to take off their pads and helmets.

Bizz felt awful. Then she had an idea. "Listen," she said excitedly. "How about if we come up with plays to use on Saturday?" The others looked up.

Encouraged, Bizz went on. "We can practice them all next week. Meet me at my house tonight, okay?" When no one replied, she added, "I'll make dessert!" There were enough nods and murmurs of "yeah, all right" to convince Bizz they were on board.

When her friends arrived that night, Bizz handed them each a brownie, a glass of milk, and a sheet of paper covered with plays she'd come up with that afternoon.

"Okay, here's the plan," she said. "Jonas and I will be forwards. Charlie, you and X are our defensemen. Mark, you'll be goalkeeper."

"What about me?" Savannah asked around a mouthful of brownie.

"There are only five players on a roller hockey team," Bizz explained. "You'll be our substitute, okay?"

Savannah looked a little disappointed, but she nodded.

X cleared his throat. "You know, I think I'd make a better forward than defenseman," he said.

"Oh," Bizz said. "Well, I guess Jonas could play back and you could —"

"No way," Jonas piped up. "You guys definitely want me on the front line. I'm the man with the moves. I'll zig when they zag, tie 'em up in circles. I'll —"

"We get the picture," Bizz said. "Listen, X, the plays I worked out call for —"

"Plays *you* worked out?" X cut in. "What about the plays *I* worked out?"

Bizz held up her hands in mock defense. "Sor-ree! I didn't know *you'd* made some plays, too. Let's see 'em." X handed over a grubby piece of paper. Bizz studied it, then put it aside. "Not bad, but the plays I came up with are better. So let's —"

X stood up. His face was angry. "Who died and made *you* captain of this team?" he demanded.

"No one!" Bizz replied, bristling. "I just figured that since I'm the one who . . . who . . ." Her voice trailed away.

"Who got us into this mess?" Mark finished helpfully.

Bizz glared at him. "I was going to say 'who wants to win the most.'"

X grabbed his paper and shoved it into his pocket. "Yeah, well, I want to win, too," he said. He sat back down and crossed his arms over his chest.

Silence filled the room. Then Savannah spoke. "What do you think Frank's team is like? 'Cause I gotta tell you, Frank seemed pretty big to me. Big — and mean. What if the rest of his team is like him?"

# CHAPTER FIVE

Everyone turned and stared at Savannah. No one, it seemed, had given much thought to the competition.

"I've never seen him at the rink before," Mark said. "I wonder where his team plays?"

Jonas snapped his fingers. "I bet I know! There's an old supermarket across town that closed two years ago. I saw some kids playing roller hockey in the parking lot there." He turned to X. "Maybe we could ride over tomorrow and scout out their team?"

"Good idea," Bizz said. "Meanwhile, the rest of us will get to the rink and start practicing."

"Make sure you sign up for the time," X said. He stood up and shrugged on his coat. "I gotta get going. Thanks for the brownies. See you guys tomorrow."

The others left soon afterward. Only after they were gone did Bizz see that no one had taken a copy of her plays. She stuffed them in her backpack for the next day.

The following morning, Bizz was at the skatepark when it opened. She hurried to the rink and jotted their names down on the sign-up sheet. They would have the rink for most of the morning.

Mark, Savannah, and Charlie showed up a few minutes later. Savannah had a brand-new mouth guard.

"Even though I'll just be subbing, I figured I'd better have it," she said.

"Good idea," said Bizz. "It'd be too bad if the puck knocked out your front teeth. Not that that would happen!" she added hurriedly when Savannah's eyes widened.

Since there were only four of them, they decided to practice passing and shooting. Bizz started with the puck. She tapped it softly to Charlie. Charlie dribbled forward a few feet. Mark came alongside him, with Bizz close on Mark's heels. Charlie flipped the puck to Mark.

"Drop pass! Drop pass!" Bizz called out.

Mark stopped. "I didn't drop it!" He lifted his stick. "The puck's right here!"

Bizz groaned. "I didn't mean you'd *dropped the pass*. I meant you should *do a drop pass*. Don't you know what that is?"

Mark shook his head. When Bizz looked at Savannah, she just shrugged.

"Oh, brother." Bizz rolled her eyes. "A drop pass is one of the most basic moves of roller hockey! How're we gonna win if you guys don't even know how to do a drop pass?" She sighed. "Good thing we have a whole week before we play. Charlie, let's show 'em how it's done."

Charlie took the puck from Mark and started to

dribble. Bizz followed behind him. When they were halfway down the rink, Charlie lifted his stick and left the puck behind for Bizz to pick up. Bizz captured it, skated the rest of the way to the goal, and shot the puck into the net.

"See?" she called as she retrieved the disk. "It's easy! And when it's done right, it can really fake out the other team."

"It's gonna take a lot more than a few good drop passes to fake *that* team out," Jonas said from behind them. "A *lot* more."

X and Jonas stood outside the rink. They looked upset. "We just checked out the competition," Jonas continued. He and X sat down at a picnic table. The others joined them.

"And?" Bizz prompted.

"And," X said, "They. Are. Big."

"How big?" Mark asked.

"Let me put it this way," Jonas said. "If the zoo reports that its gorillas are missing, I know where to find them."

# CHAPTER SIX

Bizz tried to think of something to say that would wipe the worried looks off their faces. "You know, even if they win, I'll bet they won't want to come over here to play. Why would they, when they can play on that lot?"

Jonas shook his head. "Some big department store bought the property. The construction trucks have already started ripping up one side of the lot. No way Frank and his goons will be playing hockey there anymore. And if they win on Saturday, no way they'll let *us* play hockey *here* anymore."

Bizz felt her stomach tighten. It was her fault they were in this mess. It was up to her to make sure they didn't lose. And that meant whipping them into shape — fast.

"All right," she said, getting up. "So they're bigger than us. Big deal! We can't give up without a fight. So let's go!"

Slowly, the others got up. As they skated onto the rink, Bizz said, "For the first play, let's try —"

"Hang on!" X said, frowning. "What about my plays? And we still haven't decided who's playing forward."

Bizz checked her watch. "We're losing time, here. Let's do rock-paper-scissors to see whose plays we use." X nodded.

"Rock — paper — scissors — shoot!" they chanted together. Bizz stuck out her hand, holding it flat like a piece of paper. X's hand was balled into a fist.

"Paper covers rock — I win," Bizz said. "Now do it with Jonas to see who plays forward." Jonas won and skated triumphantly to the front line.

"Now can we start practicing? Good." Bizz consulted her paper. "Mark and Savannah will be our defensemen. X and Charlie will try to keep us from scoring."

As X and Charlie skated to their positions, Bizz called the others to huddle around her. "Okay, I call this the stack play. Jonas, you start with the puck. Pass it to me right away, then skate toward the goal. Mark, you follow behind him. Savannah, you're behind Mark. I'll pass to Mark and take off for the goal. Mark does a drop pass. Savannah picks up the puck and shoots it back to me or to Jonas, whoever's got a clear shot on goal. Got it?"

Mark and Jonas nodded, but Savannah wrinkled her brow in confusion.

"Hello, Savannah!" Bizz said impatiently. "Anybody in there? Do you understand the play or not?"

Savannah looked at Bizz with hurt eyes, but she nodded.

"Then let's do it!"

They took their positions. Jonas dribbled toward the goal. X and Charlie immediately came out to double-team him. Jonas flicked the puck to Bizz. As

X and Charlie turned to attack Bizz, she shot the puck to Mark. Mark caught it. Savannah then skated up behind him. He looked over his shoulder and called out, "Ready?"

*Oh, brother,* Bizz groaned inwardly. *Why don't you just* tell *them you're going to do a drop pass?*

Sure enough, just as Mark lifted his stick, X swooped in, reached out his stick, and snagged the puck.

"Well, at least the defense is on top of things," Bizz said as she watched X take a shot on goal. "Next time, Mark, try to be a little less obvious, okay?" Mark grinned sheepishly.

"Okay, next play. Three-man weave. Simple. Jonas, you, me, and Mark line up on the center line. I've got the puck. I pass to Jonas, on my right, then skate behind him and take his spot. Jonas, you dribble to the middle, then pass to Mark. Mark takes your place, you take his. Got it?"

"What do I do?" Savannah asked.

"Stay back and out of the way," Bizz replied shortly.

# CHAPTER SEVEN

Eyes downcast, Savannah skated to a spot near the goal. Mark and Jonas exchanged glances, then took up their positions.

"Let's do it," Bizz said. She passed to Jonas, then swung around behind him. Jonas skated to the center and passed to Mark.

*So far, so g— oh no!* Bizz squeezed her eyes shut.

Instead of weaving *behind* Mark, Jonas skated in front of him. Amazingly, Mark managed to control the puck while dodging around Jonas. Now he made his way toward Bizz, getting ready to pass.

"You cover her, I'll get him!" X yelled to Charlie.

With a roar, he skated as fast as he could right at Mark.

Mark shrieked, lost his balance, and fell down. Unable to stop, X fell on top of him. The puck skittered off Mark's stick and rolled toward Savannah.

"Pick it up! Pick it up!" Bizz called. But Savannah was skating toward Mark and X.

Luckily, the boys were unharmed. "Is that your leg or mine?" X joked as they untangled themselves. They started laughing.

"All right, all right, break it up," Bizz said gruffly. Still laughing, the boys got up.

"Nice play," X commented as he dusted himself off. "A three-man weave with a two-man pileup! It'll fake 'em out for sure."

All at once, Bizz's blood boiled over. "Will you guys get serious?" she yelled. "And you," she added, turning to Savannah, "you let the puck go right by you!"

"I thought those guys were hurt!" Savannah protested.

"Who cares? If this had been a game, you could've scored when they were down! Can't you do anything right?"

Savannah stared with shocked eyes at her friend. Then she took out her mouth guard, removed her helmet, and skated out of the rink. A moment later, she disappeared into the Community Center.

"What's with her?" Bizz asked.

Mark, no longer laughing, shook his head in disgust. Without replying, he followed Savannah.

Bizz watched him go, then turned to see Charlie and X collecting their stuff. "Oh, great, you're going to quit, too?" She threw her hands up. "Jonas, help me out here!"

Jonas looked from Bizz to Charlie and X and back again. "I don't know, Bizz," he said. "I think you need more help than I can give you." He joined Charlie and X. Together, the three skated off toward the ramps and rails, leaving Bizz by herself in the empty rink.

"Fine," she muttered savagely. "Be that way. Who needs you?"

"You do," came a soft voice from behind her. Bizz whirled around and came face-to-face with Alison.

Bizz jutted out her chin. "Okay, you're right. I can't win Saturday's game all by myself."

"No, you can't," replied Alison. "But if you're not careful, by yourself is the way you're going to be — and not just this Saturday, either."

"What's that supposed to mean?"

"You're a smart girl. You'll figure it out. Hopefully, before it's too late." She skated away.

Bizz unbuckled her helmet and took off her pads. Then she picked up her mouth guard — and suddenly, she thought of Savannah. Savannah, her best friend. Savannah, who barely knew the first thing about roller hockey but was willing to play against a team of *huge* kids because her friends needed her.

And how had Bizz repaid such loyalty and bravery? By behaving like a jerk — and not just to Savannah, but to all her friends!

# CHAPTER EIGHT

Bizz gathered her things and hurried out of the park. She had a plan.

When she got home, she ran to her computer and logged on to her e-mail account. She selected her friends' names from her address book. Then she typed a letter:

Guys, I'm wicked sorry for the way I've been acting. I can't believe I made that bet without talking to you first – and then I tried to take over the team, which was totally wrong. And today, I wanted to win so much that I didn't even care if Mark and X were hurt! If you guys don't want to do the game on Saturday, I'll meet the other team and tell them we forfeit. They'll have a good time laughing at me, but I deserve it. And besides, they can't use the rink all the time, right? Maybe when they're not using it, we can play for fun, like we used to. If you want to, that is.

She pressed the send button and was about to log off when she decided to write one last note.

Savannah, I want to say a special sorry to you. Even though you don't know how to play roller hockey yet, you were right out there trying to learn enough to help out on Saturday. I think that's awesome. I hope you can forgive me, because I don't want us to stop being best friends.

That night, Bizz fell asleep wondering what school was going to be like that week. Would her friends talk to her — or would she be left alone, as she had been at the rink?

She got her answer the next morning, when she checked her e-mail before school. There was only one message. It was from Jonas.

Meet at my house tonight after dinner.

Bizz couldn't tell if it was friendly or not. Then a new e-mail, also from Jonas, came through.

I'll make dessert!

Next to his message was a smiley face.

Bizz let out a sigh of relief and logged off. As she went downstairs, she felt as if she were walking on air.

"I thought you were going to *make* dessert." Bizz sat in Jonas's kitchen, watching him scoop chocolate ice cream into bowls.

"I'm *making* it get out of the freezer and into your bowl, aren't I?" Jonas shot back.

Bizz loaded the bowls onto a tray. "Jonas?" she whispered as they headed down to the basement to join the others. "Are you sure everyone's okay with me now?"

"They're cool," he assured her. "We all thought sending an e-mail was the stand-up thing to do."

Downstairs, Bizz handed a bowl to Savannah, grabbed one for herself, and sat down next to her friend. "Thanks, amiga," Savannah whispered. "For everything." They grinned at each other.

X took a bite of ice cream and said, "My brother Brendan once told me, 'X, there is no I in t-e-a-m.'"

"So your brother can spell," Jonas said. "What's your point?"

"My point is that if we're going to win on Saturday, we have to think about what's best for the team instead of what's best for ourselves," X said. "I've been so busy trying to get everyone to look at my plays, I didn't bother to see if Bizz's were better. If they are, then they're the ones we should use."

Jonas nodded. "I've been so busy making sure I

got the position I wanted, I didn't let anybody else play forward."

"And I've been feeling hurt because I was left out," Savannah said softly. "I know I'm not a strong player — yet. It's better for the team if I sit out unless I'm absolutely needed." Bizz gave her friend a squeeze.

Everyone turned to Mark. "What?" he said, his mouth full of chocolate ice cream. "Near as I can tell, the only time I'm a problem to the team is when I fall down!"

Everyone laughed, then X said, "The point is, if we're gonna beat these guys, we gotta work together. Bizz, get out your plays!"

"I will if you will," Bizz replied.

# CHAPTER NINE

In the end, they decided that Bizz and Jonas would play forward, with X and Charlie backing them up and Mark in the goal. Midway through the game, X and Jonas would switch, "to confuse the enemy," as Jonas put it. Savannah would sub in as needed.

"But don't get too used to riding the pine," Bizz warned. "I promise to make a hockey player out of you yet!"

And she kept her word. Every day after school, Bizz coached Savannah as best she could while they all worked on plays. At the end of practice on Friday, everyone agreed that Savannah deserved the "MIP" award for Most Improved Player.

"Those guys better watch out tomorrow," Bizz observed as Savannah dodged around Mark and slammed the puck into the net, "or they won't know what hit 'em!"

Bizz was still feeling fired up the next morning. The day was clear, and the temperature was mild enough for sweatshirts instead of coats.

"Too bad," Jonas commented. "I look much bigger when I'm wearing my coat."

"I don't think it would matter," Mark said hoarsely. "Look."

Coming toward them was a group of boys. Big boys — and lots of them.

"Please tell me that's a football team that got lost on the way to a game," Savannah pleaded.

"'Fraid not," X said. "Meet the enemy."

Frank broke out of the line. "Ready to rumble?" he growled.

"Let's get this game on!" Bizz shot back.

The players took their positions, and Bizz and

Frank readied themselves for the face-off. "One of my guys will drop the puck," Frank said. He reached for the disk, but someone else grabbed it before him.

It was Alison. She had a whistle around her neck. "Thought I'd come by, make sure everyone plays an honest game." Bizz sent silent thanks to the teenager.

Alison blew her whistle and dropped the puck. Bizz stabbed it free and sent a pass to Jonas. A defenseman lunged for him. Jonas braked to a stop and fired the puck backward to X, who winged it to Bizz. She took off like a shot for the goal.

*Okay, Charlie,* she thought, *here comes the drop!* Without glancing behind her, she lifted her stick and left the puck behind. Just like they'd practiced, Charlie snagged the disk. He dodged around one defenseman and flicked a pass up the rink to where Bizz was waiting.

Without hesitation, Bizz slapped the puck toward the goal. The shot felt good, but the puck ricocheted off a post. Bizz dashed forward to retrieve it. The goalkeeper got to it first and sent it spinning to his

teammate. A few quick passes later, the puck was in the net behind Mark. Score: one to zero.

"Let's get it back!" Bizz called to her teammates.

Alison dropped the puck for the face-off. This time, Frank won control. He made a beeline for the goal. His teammates roared down with him. With a series of quick passes, they drove past X and Charlie. Mark didn't stand a chance. The puck hit the net, and the score was two–zip.

As Bizz skated back to her spot, she whispered to her teammates, "If I get the puck, three-man weave. Me, X, and Jonas." The others nodded.

After a brief battle of jabbing sticks, Bizz came away with the puck. Jonas flew up one side of the rink, looking for a pass. But X was undefended, so Bizz flicked the puck to him. Using short, sharp passes and quick turns, the three wove toward the goal. Moments later, Bizz slapped a shot — score!

Bizz raised her arms in triumph.

*Slam!*

Someone hit her from behind! She crashed to the ground, landing hard on her leg. Her teammates clustered around. "Sorry, guys," Bizz said weakly. "I'm out. Guess that means we lose."

"Says who?"

# CHAPTER TEN

Savannah took her mouth guard from her pocket and shoved it into her mouth.

"Savannah, these guys are really good. Are you sure?" Bizz asked.

Savannah tossed her hair. "I'm sure."

Bizz's teammates helped her to the picnic table. Jonas fetched an ice pack from the Community Center. Meanwhile, Alison sent the boy who hit Bizz to the sidelines. Then she skated up to Bizz.

"You okay?" she asked. Bizz nodded. "That hit from behind earns your team a penalty shot. Who do you want to take it?"

Penalty shots were tough. The puck was placed in

the face-off circle. The shooter had one chance to get the puck past the goalie. If that one shot didn't make it in, too bad. But if it did . . .

Bizz looked at her teammates. A goal now would even up the score, giving them a fighting chance at victory. X and Jonas could probably do it. She wasn't sure about Charlie or Mark.

Then she turned to Savannah — and smiled. "You take it," she said to her friend. Savannah looked startled, but she skated to the face-off circle without arguing. Alison placed the puck before her, stepped back, and blew her whistle. The goalie crouched in the crease. Savannah raised her stick behind her and swung.

*Thwack!*

The puck soared toward the goal. Bizz held her breath as the goalie lunged forward, reached out his glove — and just managed to knock the puck away. As the other team cheered, Savannah slowly skated back to her friends.

"I blew it," she said sadly.

"Are you kidding me?" Bizz cried. "Do you know how difficult penalty shots are? And he almost didn't stop it! Not bad for someone who's only been playing for one week." She grinned at Savannah. "Now get out there. They can't win that game without you!"

Savannah hugged Bizz and skated to her position on defense. X moved to the front line with Jonas. Charlie and Mark took up their same spots — and the game was on.

Back and forth went the action. Jonas and X worked well together on the front line. Between them, they scored three goals. Savannah did her best on defense, clearing the puck to the side whenever it came loose near her. Charlie teamed up with the front line for some plays and stayed back on others. And Mark saved almost as many goals as he let in.

Almost, but not quite. When Alison blew her whistle to signal the end of the game, the score was uneven. Frank's team had won seven to four. They celebrated by making woofing noises and rolling

upraised fists through the air. Then, after shouting "loo-oo-sers!" a few times, they left the park.

Alison made sure Bizz's leg was okay, then she left, too.

The kids sat around the picnic table.

"I can't believe we lost," Jonas said. "No more rink, no more hockey."

"Shoot, we can still play," Bizz said. "We'll find a place. And we'll get better until our team totally rocks! And when we do," she finished, her voice full of determination, "we'll challenge those guys to a rematch. So, who's with me?"

She put her hand in the middle of the table. Savannah laid her hand on top, followed by Charlie, X, Jonas, and Mark. They grinned at one another, then, with a *whoop*, flung their hands into the air.

"Go, team!"

# Roller Hockey Safety

Roller hockey is a fast-paced, action-filled sport. To play roller hockey, you need to know how to inline skate and how to handle a hockey stick. You also need to have the proper safety equipment.

Worried that such equipment will slow you down? Think you're too tough to need it? Think again!

Roller hockey is played on pavement. Roller hockey players move quickly. Imagine a fast-moving player falling down on pavement or colliding with another player. If he or she isn't wearing protective gear, he or she is going to get badly hurt.

Roller hockey pucks are made of hard rubber. When a puck is hit forcefully, it flies at great speed. If it strikes a player, it can do serious damage unless the player is wearing the proper gear.

Therefore, it's important for roller hockey players to protect themselves from the top down. Helmets with face masks; mouth guards; wrist guards; and elbow, knee, and shin pads are worn by all players. Goalies wear even more padding. Long-sleeve shirts and lightweight pants can help prevent scrapes.

After all, you've only got one body – so use your brain and protect it!